the MOST PERFECT SNOWMAN

by CHRIS BRITT

BALZER + BRAY

An Imprint of HarperCollins *Publishers*

Balzer + Bray is an imprint of HarperCollins Publishers.

The Most Perfect Snowman
Copyright © 2016 by Chris Britt
All rights reserved. Manufactured in China.

Library of Congress Control Number: 2015951328
ISBN 978-0-06-237704-3

The artist used watercolor, acrylic, Tombow pencils H, HB, and 4H to create the illustrations for this book.
Typography by Dana Fritts
16 17 18 19 20 SCP 10 9 8 7 6 5 4 3 2 1
❖
First Edition

TO MY DAUGHTER, EMILY,
THE BUILDER OF THE MOST
PERFECT SNOWMEN

Drift was the loneliest of snowmen.
Made from the first blustery snow of winter,
he'd been built fast and then forgotten . . .

with only two skinny stick arms,
and a small mouth
and eyes made of coal.

Drift dreamed of wearing a stylish hat, scarf, and mittens just like the other snowmen. Most of all, he dreamed of having a pointy orange carrot nose.

"If only I had that, I'd be perfect," he thought.

All the other snowmen were much fancier than Drift and would giggle at him with frosty glee.

Dressed in their finery, they would have snowy fashion parades,

snowball fights,

and snowman dances that lasted all night.

But Drift was never included.

So he spent his days alone, swooshing and sliding through the wintry woods,

often stopping in the shadows to watch
the others laugh and play.

One morning, three bundled-up children walked by.

"What a plain-looking snowman!" said one little girl. "You need a hat. Here, take mine."

The hat was blue, fluffy, and toasty warm. It fit perfectly!

"And you can have my mittens," said the little boy.

They were so snuggly! Drift raised his arms in the air and smiled.

The last little girl turned to Drift. "Why don't you take my scarf."
It felt soft and cozy as she placed it around his neck.

She looked at him for a moment. "Hmmm, you're still missing something."

Then, reaching into her coat pocket . . .

she pulled out the most pointy orange carrot nose that Drift had ever seen!

She squashed it into place.

NOW YOU'RE THE PERFECT SNOWMAN!

The other snowmen watched in astonishment.

All afternoon Drift played with the children.
He had never been so happy.

But soon, dark clouds rolled in, and his new friends turned to walk back home. Drift thanked them and waved good-bye.

That night, a terrible blizzard began to blow. Icy snowflakes ripped at Drift's new hat and mittens and tossed them into the air. "Oh no!" Drift gasped.

"Oh well." Drift sighed. "At least I still have my beautiful new scarf and nose."

Then, through the howling wind, Drift heard a whisper-soft voice.

"I'm lost. Can you help me please?"

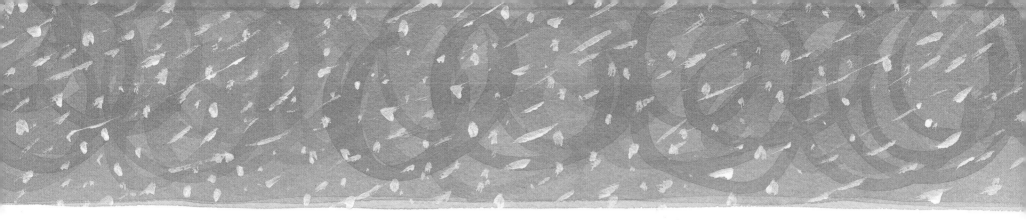

It was a tiny bunny. It looked frightened and shivery cold.

The bunny needed a safe place to survive the night. But there was no shelter to be found.

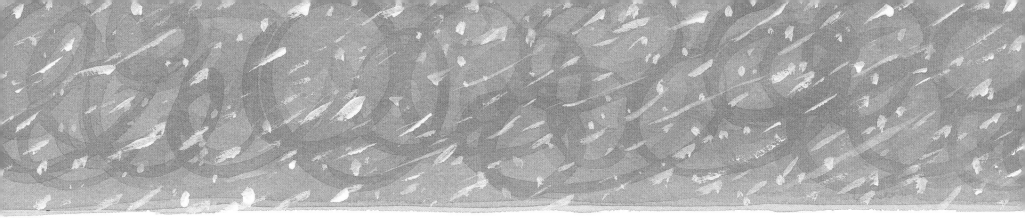

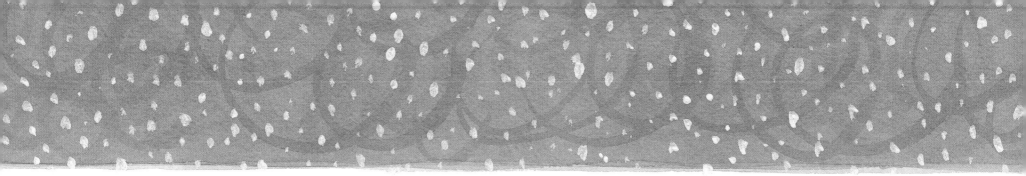

Drift took off his scarf and wrapped it gently around the bunny.

"There! Now you'll stay warm."

That's when he heard a faint growl.
It was the bunny's tummy!

RUMBLE

Drift stared into the frosty night.
He knew what he had to do.

He reached up, removed
his last remaining gift,

and gave his new friend something to eat.

And became the most perfect snowman of all.